Abby Invents

Unbreakable Crayons

Purchase additional titles at www.abbyinvents.com

To my nieces and nephews:
Dream big. Always, in all ways.

To Miss Almeida's Grade 4 Class:
Your feedback was valuable! Thank you!
Abby thanks you, too!

"Class, meet Inventor Maya Smartt!" said Miss Pilar.
Abby gasped, "She looks like me."

"I built a robot that helps kids with their homework. I named it TutorMe Bot," said Inventor Maya.

SNAP! Abby's crayon broke in two.

One by one, all the other students' crayons broke too.

"Not again!" she groaned.

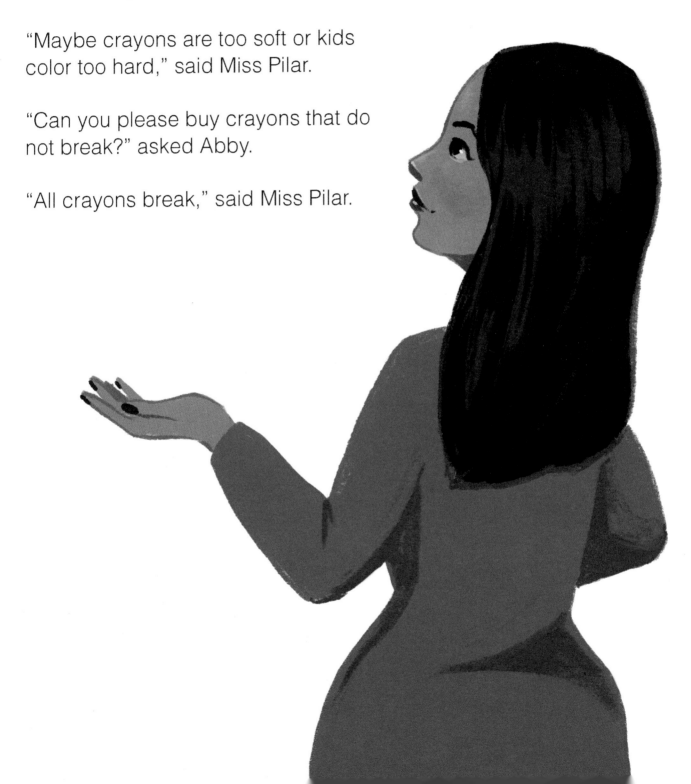

"Miss Pilar, **ALL** the crayons broke again!! Why do they always break?" asked Abby.

"Maybe crayons are too soft or kids color too hard," said Miss Pilar.

"Can you please buy crayons that do not break?" asked Abby.

"All crayons break," said Miss Pilar.

WHAT?

All crayons break?

"There isn't one crayon in the whole, wide world that doesn't break?!" asked Abby.

"No, all crayons break." said Miss Pilar.

Abby grumbled.

Then, she had a brilliant idea.

"I will make the first Unbreakable Crayons."

Miss Pilar smiled,

"You are a problem solver. You are an Inventor. You solve problems, big and small, because you have great ideas."

Abby was bursting with questions.

WHAT are crayons made of?
HOW are crayons made?
WHY do crayons break?

After school, she marched to the library.
She learned that crayons are made of wax and dye.
Wax makes crayons hard. Dyes give crayons their color.

The Crayon

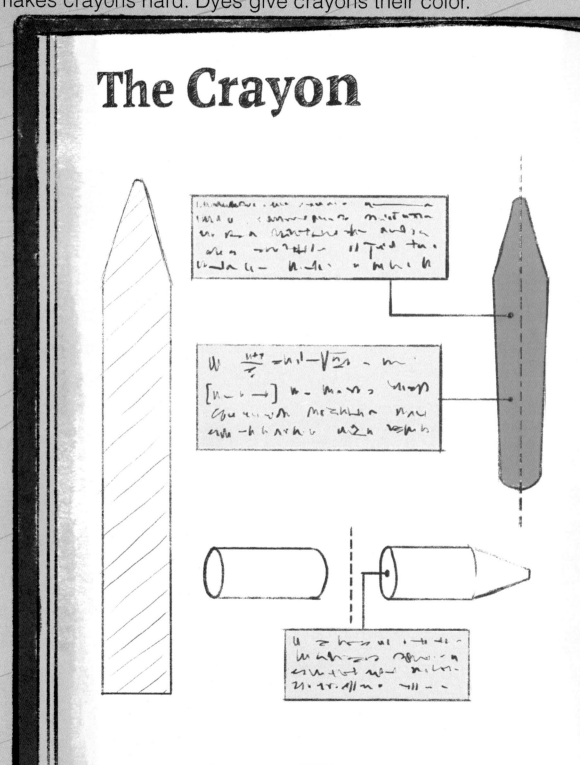

Next, she learned how crayons are made.

1. Heat the wax until it melts.

2. Blend the wax with a dye.

3. Pour the mixture into a machine that has holes, shaped like crayons.

4. Cool the mixture until it turns solid.

5. The machine will pop out wax crayons.

Finally, she learned why crayons break.
Crayons break because they are not strong enough. They are thin and long so if pressed too hard, they will break. Miss Pilar was right.

The Unbreakable CRAYON

Abby sketched her Unbreakable Crayons. They must be...

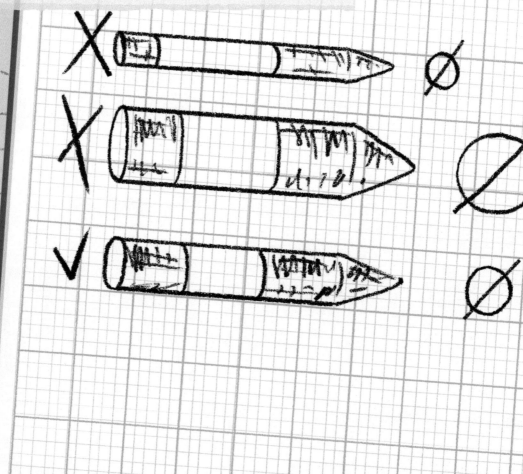

Not too thin, not too thick.

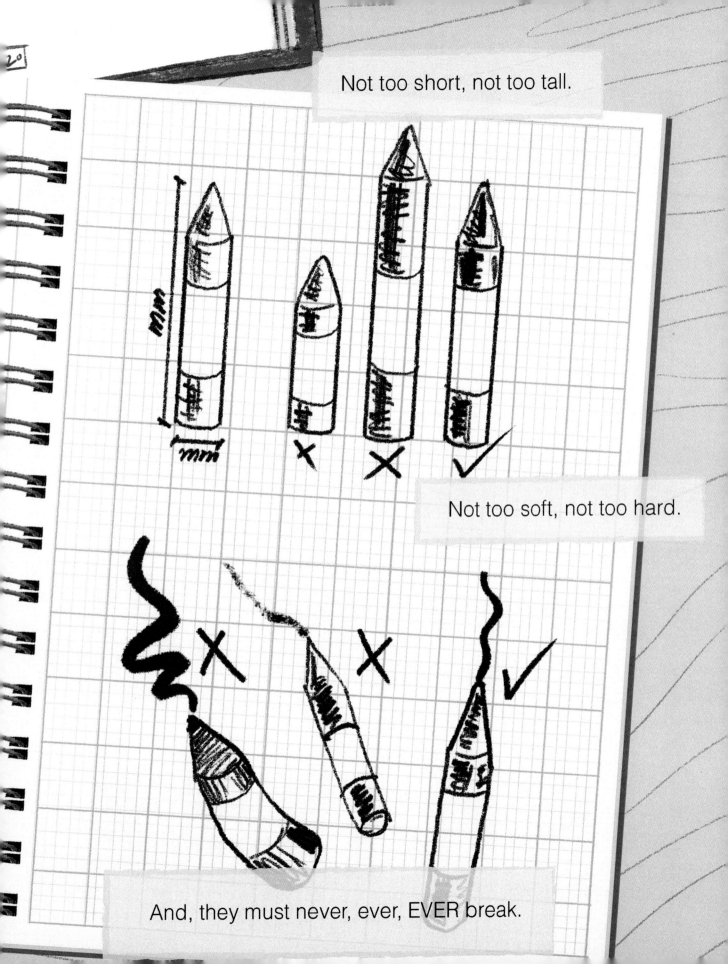

Miss Pilar helped Abby carry out tests in the school's lab.

"Safety first!" warned Miss Pilar. "Wear a lab coat and safety glasses, please."

On the first try, all the crayons broke.

Abby tried again.

She added plenty dye sometimes.

She added a tiny drop of dye other times.

She baked longer sometimes. She cooled faster other times.

Still, the crayons kept breaking.

"Grrrr! Arrrgh!" yelled Abby.
"I give up. This is too hard!!"

"Oh Abby, remember what Inventor Maya told you," said Miss Pilar.

"Your tests will fail many times, but you cannot quit. Can you think of everyday items that do not break?"

Abby went to the playground.

She watched kids play on the swings and monkey bars.

She took out her notepad and wrote, "Things that DO NOT break (at the playground)."

1. Swing seats

2. Monkey bars

3. Slides

She ran to see Miss Pilar at the lab.

"What are swing seats made of?"

- HARD PLASTIC

"What are monkey bars made of?"

- HARD PLASTIC

"What are slides made of?"

- HARD PLASTIC

Perhaps the secret to Unbreakable Crayons was

HARD PLASTIC, not wax.

Abby and Miss Pilar grinned.

"I am a problem solver.
I am an Inventor.
I solve problems, big and small,
Because I have great ideas,"
sang Abby.

Abby tried again.
She added plenty dye sometimes.
She added a tiny drop of dye other times.

She baked longer sometimes.

She cooled faster other times.

After two long weeks, Abby created the perfect recipe.

1. Heat hard plastic until it melts

2. Add Colored Dye and stir

3. Pour mixture into a crayon mold with round holes

4. Bake in oven
for one hour

5. Cool until mixture
turns solid

6. Out pops
UNBREAKABLE CRAYONS!

To test how hard her Unbreakable Crayons were, Abby jumped on them.

They didn't break.

She bent them.

They didn't break.

Miss Pilar EVEN drove the school bus over them.

Still, they didn't break.

Abby shared the Unbreakable Crayons with her classmates.

"Whoa! These are strong crayons!" said one of the students.

Thanks to Abby's invention, no one had to worry about broken crayons anymore.

Abby wrote a letter to Inventor Maya.

Dear Inventor Maya,

Thank you for speaking at
Miss Pilar's class. I am now
an inventor, just like you! 😊
I invented Unbreakable
Crayons. I am sending you a
few to try. Happy coloring!

Inventor Abby

The next year, Abby got a patent from the government.
It is a certificate that says she was the first person, in the
entire country, to create Unbreakable Crayons.

"I cannot wait to invent again!" smiled Abby.

"Inventing is so much fun."

Hello Future Inventor!

Thank you for reading my book! This is what I looked like when I was about your age. I never imagined that I would become an inventor, but I did. You can be an inventor, too! Yes, you! If Abby & I can do it, you can too.

You are a problem solver. You are an inventor. You solve problems big and small because you have great ideas! I CANNOT wait to see what you invent. I know it's going to be cool.

I hope you enjoyed reading Abby's story as much as I enjoyed writing it. I welcome your feedback — please leave a review on AbbyInvents.com (my online store), Amazon or Goodreads.

Stay curious,

Dr. Arlyne Simon

P. S. If you liked this book, you may like Abby Invents The Foldibot. Visit www.abbyinvents.com for additional titles, coloring & activity pages.

THE END

GLOSSARY

1. Invent – to make or design something that never existed before.

2. Inventor – The first person to make or design a new device, machine or process.

3. Invention – a new process or device that did not exist before.

4. Patent – a document given to an inventor, by the government which prevents other people from making, selling or using the invention for up to twenty years.

ear Future Inventor ————————————————————,

(write your name here)

. Inventor Abby replaced wax with hard plastic to create
nbreakable Crayons. But, this is not the only way to prevent
rayons from breaking. What would you invent to prevent your
rayons from breaking? Draw your inventions below.

2. Do you have ideas for other inventions? Draw your
inventions below. Describe how you will design your inventions.
And, keep your notes safe to protect your idea. Someday, you
may also get a patent from the government.

Made in the USA
Monee, IL
30 June 2023

38187867R00024